BL: 3.9 ARpts: 1

Get to know the girls of

SLEEP-OVER!

BY
ROWAN McAULEY

ILLUSTRATED BY
ASH OSWALD

SQUARE
FISH

FEIWEL AND FRIENDS
NEW YORK

SQUARE
FISH

An Imprint of Macmillan
175 Fifth Avenue
New York, NY 10010
mackids.com

Our books may be purchased in bulk for promotional,
educational, or business use. Please contact your local
bookseller or the Macmillan Corporate and Premium Sales
Department at (800) 221-7945 ext. 5442 or by e-mail at
MacmillanSpecialMarkets@macmillan.com.

Library of Congress Cataloging-in-Publication Data Available

ISBN 978-1-250-09812-2

First published in Australia by E2,
an imprint of Hardie Grant Egmont.
Illustration and design by Ash Oswald.

First published in the United States by Feiwel and Friends
First Square Fish Edition: 2013
Square Fish Reissue Edition: 2016
Square Fish logo designed by Filomena Tuosto

1   3   5   7   9   10   8   6   4   2

AR: 3.9

CHAPTER
❀ ONE

It was six o'clock on Friday morning, the last day of school for the year. The alarm hadn't gone off yet, but Olivia was already awake, dressed, and sitting at the kitchen table, eating her toast and waiting for her mom to get up.

She drank a glass of milk and ate an apple, but her mom still slept on. She brushed her teeth and made her lunch, but even then her mom did not stir.

Olivia checked the clock on the microwave. Six thirty. Surely her mom should be awake by now? She tiptoed along the hallway and looked in. Her mom was fast asleep, snoring slightly. Olivia knocked gently on the open door. Her mom did not move.

Olivia cleared her throat, "Ahem!"

Her mom rolled over in bed and snored more loudly. Olivia was getting desperate.

"Mom," she whispered.

"Mom," she said gently.

"Mom!" she said more firmly.

This was getting her nowhere.

"MOM!" she yelled suddenly and stamped her foot.

"Hmm?" said her mom, sitting up in bed, her hair all fluffy on one side. "What's up, baby?"

"Mom," said Olivia. "You have to get up. I am sleeping over at Ching Ching's house tonight."

"Are you?" said her mom. "Are you sure? Did we talk about this?"

"Mom," said Olivia sternly, because she had to be strict with her mom sometimes. "You know it is. We talked about it on Monday, remember? You spoke with Mrs. Adams on the phone."

"I know, baby," said her mom,

yawning. "I'm just teasing you."

"Well," said Olivia, "will you get up now?"

"Mmm," said her mom, still sounding tired. "What time is it?"

"Six thirty," said Olivia. "Or even later by now. We've been talking for at least five minutes."

"Six thirty?"

"Or six thirty-five," said Olivia.

"Is the sun even up yet?" asked her mom.

"Mom!"

"OK, OK," said her mom. "I'm getting up. Even though it's still the middle of the night," she grumbled.

"Come on," said Olivia. "Here's your bathrobe."

Hurry UP, Mom, I'll be late!

While her mom took a shower, Olivia checked her bag again. As well as her lunchbox, she had packed her pajamas, her swimsuit, some clean clothes for tomorrow, her hairbrush, and a small box of chocolates for Ching Ching's mom, to say thank you. Was that everything?

It was almost seven o'clock and Olivia was dancing with impatience, waiting for her mom to finish blow-drying her hair. Finally, she was ready.

"OK," she said to Olivia. "Now, are you sure you have packed everything you need?"

"Yes," said Olivia.

"Pajamas?"

"Yes," said Olivia.

"Chocolates for Mrs. Adams?"

"Yes," said Olivia.

"Clean underwear for tomorrow?"

"Mom!"

"Well, have you?"

"YES!" said Olivia. "Come on!"

"All right!" said her mom. "Just checking.

I'll just get the keys. . . . "

But Olivia was already out the door and waiting at the front gate, her backpack on her back. Her mom locked the door and walked down the path (so slowly!), and together they walked to the bus stop.

"I'm going to miss you tonight," said her mom.

"Yeah, yeah," said Olivia, looking ahead for the bus.

"I will. I won't see you all day, I won't have anyone to eat dinner with, and you'll be at Ching Ching's until tomorrow. . . . "

"I know," said Olivia.

"What time am I picking you up?"

"Lunchtime," said Olivia. "Ching Ching

and I will have breakfast together, and play in the morning, and then you can pick me up at lunchtime."

"Lunchtime it is," said her mom, giving her a hug and a big smoochy kiss.

The bus was just arriving at the corner.

"Bye, mom," said Olivia, yelling back over her shoulder as she ran to catch it.

At last she was on her way.

CHAPTER TWO

On the bus, Olivia tried to relax. She looked out the window and noticed how few cars there were on the road. She looked around the bus and saw all the empty seats. She wasn't going to be late at all. In fact, she was early.

It felt funny to sit on the same old bus, wearing her same old school uniform, and carrying her same old backpack, knowing that inside the bag were her pink-and-green pajamas. What if she got to school and Mrs. Delano asked her to fetch something and she accidentally pulled out her new blue underwear instead?

She would die!

Or what if somebody found the box of chocolates for Ching Ching's mom and ate them, and she had nothing to give her? Or what if . . .

Olivia was not very good at relaxing.

By the time the bus arrived outside school, she was exhausted. She had thought up a hundred different disasters and had worried about each and every one, and it wasn't even eight o'clock yet.

Olivia dragged her bag off the bus. She was starting to feel slightly sick.

Maybe it wasn't such a good idea to sleep over at Ching Ching's, even though they were best friends. What if she and Ching Ching had a fight and they weren't even friends by the time her mom came to pick them up from school? Maybe she should tell Ching Ching that she had changed her mind. She could just give the chocolates to Ching Ching, and then phone her mom and say she would come home for dinner after all.

Across the playground, she saw Ching Ching waving at her, a huge smile on her face. Ching Ching's mom was a teacher and her dad was the principal, so Ching Ching and her brothers were always at school early.

"Hi, Olivia!" said Ching Ching, running over. "Isn't tonight going to be cool?"

"Yeah," said Olivia, running to meet her halfway. "It's going to be the best!"

She gave Ching Ching a hug and threw

her bag under a tree, and they went to play
with the other kids until the bell rang.

The last day of school always dragged
on forever. Everyone was itching to get
out and be on vacation, but first they had
to empty their lockers, tidy up the class-
room, and collect all the art they had
done that year.

Nobody could concentrate.

Dylan kept pestering Mrs. Delano,
asking, "But why, miss? It's the last day of
school. Can't we just play?"

By lunchtime, Mrs. Delano had given up.

"OK," she said. "You win. We've done enough and it's too hot to work anyway."

So they spent the rest of the day singing and talking about what everyone was doing for the holidays.

When it was time to leave, everyone was lined up and ready to go. Bags on their shoulders, they crowded at the school gates, straining their ears for the bell.

Come on, bell! RING!

"There it is!" yelled someone, and they were off, flying out to freedom. Some ran to buses, and others went up the hill to the train station. Some walked home, and some, like Olivia and Ching Ching, waited to be picked up.

Ching Ching's parents both worked at the high school where Ching Ching's brothers went. Ching Ching was adopted and didn't look anything like her brothers. They were big, loud boys, all with the same short, spiky blond hair. Their names were Henry, Daniel, and William.

Olivia had met them lots of times before, of course. The first time had been at Ching Ching's birthday party at the zoo.

The boys were funny and rough, and had teased Ching Ching, picking her up and carrying her around the zoo, shouting to one another.

"Throw her to the seals!"

"No—too little! Not enough for a seal to eat. Here—catch!"

And Daniel had thrown—actually *thrown*—Ching Ching to Henry. Olivia had been astonished, watching her friend sail through the air like a doll. And Henry had caught her and called to William, "Should we chuck her to the monkeys?"

"Yeah!" said William. "She looks like a monkey."

"Smells like one, too," said Daniel.

"Let's go!" said Henry, and all three boys had carried Ching Ching away, hooting and chattering like monkeys as they went.

Olivia had been so upset, she was nearly in tears. How could they be so horrible to Ching Ching? And on her birthday!

But Ching Ching had come back giggling, sitting on William's shoulders, and waving to everyone.

So they weren't bad boys, exactly. It's just that Olivia didn't have any brothers and wasn't quite sure what to make of them.

CHAPTER THREE

"Hey!" said Ching Ching. "There they are!"

She pointed to a car slowly driving by, looking for somewhere to park. Olivia could see that it was full of Ching Ching's brothers. Ching Ching's mom waved her hand out the driver's window.

"Come on," said Ching Ching, and they ran to the car.

Mrs. Adams parked the car a long, long

way up the street from the school. Ching Ching and Olivia were puffing by the time they got there.

It was a hot summer afternoon, and their backpacks were heavy with all the things they had brought home from their desks and lockers. Olivia had her clothes for the sleepover, too, so her bag was bulging at its zipper.

Henry was sitting up front next to Mrs. Adams, and Daniel and William and their backpacks were filling the backseat, so Ching Ching and Olivia decided to sit in the special backwards-facing seats in the hatchback.

Olivia loved sitting back there, watching

the traffic come towards them, waving to the drivers in the cars behind as they waited at the lights. Mrs. Adams opened the back and helped them climb in.

"Hello, Olivia," she said, after kissing Ching Ching.

"Hello, Mrs. Adams," said Olivia.

"Now," said Mrs. Adams, "did you remember everything?"

Standing behind her, Ching Ching rolled her eyes at Olivia. Olivia tried not to laugh.

"Yes, I think so," said Olivia.

"Your pajamas?" said Mrs. Adams.

"Yes."

"Your toothbrush?"

"Ye—" Olivia began, but then stopped.

Her hand covered her mouth. Her eyes were as round as saucers. She felt herself blushing from her neck to her hair. She was horrified—she had forgotten her toothbrush.

"Oh, no," she said sadly.

"That's OK," said Mrs. Adams. "I have

to stop at some stores on the way home anyway. We'll buy you a toothbrush there."

"I'm so sorry," said Olivia.

"It's no problem," said Mrs. Adams. "You jump in with Ching Ching and we'll be off."

Olivia was miserable. She had messed up her sleepover with Ching Ching even before they got to her house. How could she be so forgetful? How could she have left her toothbrush behind? She had been so careful with everything else. She felt like crying.

"Don't worry," said Ching Ching. "I always forget my toothbrush. That's why my mom asked."

But it was so embarrassing and Olivia couldn't be cheered up. If only she knew that things were about to get worse!

CHAPTER FOUR

Mrs. Adams pulled into the parking lot, and all the kids streamed out. She sent Henry and William to the farmer's market to buy some potatoes, green beans, and broccoli. She sent Daniel to the supermarket for milk and rice, and she went with the girls to the pharmacy to pick up some pills for Mr. Adams and a toothbrush for Olivia. Ching Ching found a purple one with stars.

"You have to get this one, Mom," she said. "Please? I have a pink one like this and now Olivia and I can have the same."

So Mrs. Adams bought the toothbrush and they met the boys back at the butcher's. When the butcher saw them all standing there—Henry and William with the vegetables, Daniel with the milk and rice, and Mrs. Adams with the girls—he looked amazed and said, "What a lot of children!"

He leaned over the counter and smiled at Olivia.

"And you're having a friend over to play! Aren't you lucky!" he said.

Oh, this was bad! Too, too terrible.

Olivia looked at Mrs. Adams and her

long, blonde hair and light blue eyes. She looked at Henry, Daniel, and William. They had blond hair and light blue eyes, too.

She looked at Ching Ching with her shiny black hair and dark brown eyes and realized that to strangers, Ching Ching did not look like she belonged. Instead, the butcher thought Olivia was Mrs. Adams's daughter and Ching Ching was just a friend.

This was much, much worse than forgetting her toothbrush. Worse even than the thought of Henry, Daniel, and William accidentally seeing her underwear.

She looked sideways at Ching Ching to see if she was angry, or if she was as upset and embarrassed as Olivia was, but Ching

Ching was looking at her mom with an odd smile on her face.

Mrs. Adams looked at the butcher and said, "What?!"

Mrs. Adams hugged Ching Ching tightly to her.

"Only this one is mine," she said loudly. "I don't know where the rest of them came from."

Ching Ching giggled in her mom's arms.

"Really?" said the butcher, looking surprised.

"Yes, it's true," said Henry. "We're all adopted, except for Ching Ching."

"Oh," said the butcher. "Well. What can I get you?"

"Three pounds of sausage, please," said Mrs. Adams.

Back in the car, Olivia whispered to Ching Ching, "That was awful."

"Oh, we don't care," laughed Ching Ching. "It happens all the time. Mom made it into a game and now the boys compete to see who can say the silliest thing with a straight face. Henry always wins, of course."

CHAPTER FIVE

Ching Ching's house was very different from Olivia's. At home, it was just Olivia and her mom. They lived in a small apartment. They had one bedroom each, a living room where they had their dinner at the coffee table in front of the TV, and a balcony where they hung their laundry and grew herbs in pots. Everything was crowded, but very neat.

Ching Ching's house was much bigger. There were four bedrooms. One for Mr. and Mrs. Adams, one for Henry, one that Daniel and William shared, and one for Ching Ching.

They had a huge kitchen and living room, and a big backyard with trees and a swimming pool.

There was lots of space, but everything was untidy and cluttered. There were books and papers on every surface, footballs and tennis balls and sneakers all over the place, coffee mugs and pencil cases and calculators and toys, and even pieces of cold toast. It was a mess!

Olivia loved it. She was a quiet girl, but

secretly she loved all the noise and chaos of Ching Ching's house.

At her house, Olivia would have some fruit and yogurt for an afternoon snack, and then she would do her homework until her mom came home from work. Then they'd cook dinner together and watch TV.

At Ching Ching's house, Mrs. Adams gave them cookies and sponge cake for an

This is the life!

afternoon snack and sent them all outside. The boys played soccer and Olivia and Ching Ching swam in the pool until Mr. Adams came home from being principal.

Then they all sat down to dinner at the dining table. Olivia's mom cooked spicy things like chili beans and curry, and they served up dinner straight from the pots on the stove. If Olivia wanted seconds, she had to go back to the kitchen.

Mrs. Adams cooked very different food in enormous pots. The food was laid out on the table in serving dishes and everyone helped themselves. That night, they were having sausage, mashed potatoes, beans, and broccoli.

The mashed potatoes were OK, and Olivia was used to beans and broccoli, but her mom never cooked sausage. Olivia really didn't like sausage, but Mrs. Adams put some on her plate without asking, and now she had to eat it.

She looked around the table. Mr. Adams and Henry were putting barbeque sauce on their sausage. Mrs. Adams was sprinkling hers with salt and pepper. Ching Ching was having ketchup.

"Do you want some?" she asked Olivia.

"Yes, please," said Olivia.

She liked ketchup, and maybe if she had enough of it, she could get through the sausage. She took the bottle from

Ching Ching. It was a big bottle, but it was nearly empty and the ketchup was taking forever to trickle out. Olivia shook it gently over her plate.

Nothing.

She shook it again.

"Where's the ketchup?" said Daniel.

"Olivia's using it," said Ching Ching.

"Hurry up," said Daniel, rolling his eyes.

Olivia blushed. She could feel everyone looking at her and the stupid bottle of ketchup. The ketchup still hadn't come out.

"Daniel," said Mr. Adams. "Don't be so rude. Take your time, Olivia. Daniel's in no hurry."

"Yes, I am," said Daniel. "I'm starving.

Look, just give the bottle a good thump," he said to Olivia.

Olivia wished she'd never come. Or that Daniel would be quiet. Or at the very least, that the ketchup would come out!

She hit the bottle hard, and then— SPLAT!

A huge dollop of ketchup spurted out of the bottle all over her plate, making a disgusting sound. It covered all three sausages, all the beans, and most of the mashed potatoes.

"Oh, come on!" said Daniel. "Have you left any for us?"

"Daniel!" said Mr. Adams. "Enough!"

Ching Ching poked her tongue out at

her brother. Olivia passed him the ketchup, not even looking at him.

"But, Dad," said Daniel, "you never let us have that much ketchup. You always say we can only have a dab."

Olivia just wanted to disappear.

Dinner was a disaster.

She tried to pretend that she liked having great pools of ketchup all over her food. She cut up the first sausage and ate a piece. It was dripping with ketchup. *It's not too bad*, she told herself.

The boys were talking to their dad, and Ching Ching was telling her mom about school, so no one was left to talk to Olivia. Good. She kept her head down and worked through the sausage, covering each bite in ketchup.

By the time she finished her dinner, she felt ill. She never wanted to taste ketchup again. Her throat was burning with it. More than anything in the world, Olivia wanted her mom to phone up and say she needed Olivia back home right away.

"Has everyone had enough to eat?" said Mrs. Adams.

"That was great," said Mr. Adams.

William groaned and patted his belly. Henry burped.

"Henry!" said Mrs. Adams. "Olivia, dear, would you like some more?"

Olivia shook her head firmly. *No way*, she thought.

"I mean, no thanks," she said, trying to sound polite.

"OK, then," said Mrs. Adams. "Clear the table."

The Adams had no television, but they did have a dishwasher. After dinner, each person rinsed their own plate and stacked it in the dishwasher.

When the table was cleared, Mrs. Adams brought a tub of ice cream and a package of waffle cones to the table.

"One ice cream cone each," she said. "And you can eat them outside."

She made up the cones and passed them one by one along the table.

"Now, shoo!" she said. "I need some peace and quiet."

CHAPTER SIX

Outside, it was still light. The sun was setting, though, and the sky was pink and orange over the trees.

Henry, Daniel, and William ate their ice cream as fast as they could and went back to playing soccer. Ching Ching and Olivia made their ice cream last as long as possible and then decided to go for another swim.

"It's so nice to swim as it gets dark," said Ching Ching. "The water's so warm, and you can just lie on your back and watch the birds go by and the stars come out."

Olivia agreed. They paddled and talked and looked at the sky and, except for the boys shouting as they played soccer, it was very peaceful.

After a while, it was too dark for the boys to see the ball and they packed up and went back inside. It was really quiet by the pool now, and a tiny bit spooky.

"Do you ever think," said Olivia, "you could just sink under the water and never come up?"

"Yeah," said Ching Ching. "You could

swim so deep you got sucked down that
big drain."

They shuddered happily at the thought.
They did this sometimes—talked about
scary things to see how much they could
frighten themselves.

"And the next day, there'd be nothing

but your pigtail stuck in the pool filter," said Olivia.

"And then one foot would be washed up on a beach, miles and miles away," said Ching Ching.

"Eeew!" they said together, laughing, but holding on tight to the edge of the pool, just in case.

"We should sleep out here tonight," said Ching Ching.

"Yeah?" said Olivia. "What about mosquitoes?"

"We would sleep right under the sheets," said Ching Ching. "Maybe we could burn one of those smelly candles, too."

"And we could stay up all night and watch the sun rise," said Olivia.

"Ching Ching!"

It was Mrs. Adams calling from the backdoor.

"Time for bed. You and Olivia, out of the pool, now!"

"You can *so* tell your mom is a teacher," said Olivia.

They got out of the pool and found that their fingers and toes had gotten wrinkly. The air was cool on their wet skin and by the time they got inside, they were shivering.

They stood together in front of the bathroom mirror with their matching toothbrushes, giggling and trying to brush their chattering teeth. They brushed their hair and Ching Ching tied hers back in long, low braids for bed. They changed into their pajamas and decided it was too much effort to sleep outside that night.

Ching Ching had bunk beds, and because it was the first time Olivia had slept over, she got to sleep on top.

"I always read for a while before I go to sleep," said Ching Ching. "Would you like to borrow a book, or do you have one?"

"Borrow one, please," said Olivia, because Ching Ching always had lots of books. Olivia supposed it was because both her parents worked at the school.

Olivia found one about a girl who ran

away to sea on a pirate ship. It looked very interesting, but when she climbed up the ladder to her bed and got in under the covers, she didn't feel like reading.

At home, in her own bed, her mom usually came in and kissed her good night. Sometimes they talked about their day, sometimes Olivia read out loud from a book, and sometimes her mom told her a story instead. She remembered how her mom had said that morning that she would miss Olivia.

Olivia realized this was the first time in her life she had gone to bed without even a hug from her mom. She felt a bit sad and lonely.

Outside in the pool, talking with Ching Ching, Olivia had forgotten all about the embarrassment of dinner. Now, lying in bed, she started thinking about it all over again. She felt her stomach shrink into a cold, hard ball.

It was too late to call her mom and ask to go home. She was stuck here. Daniel was horrible, Mrs. Adams probably thought she

was silly for forgetting her toothbrush, and everyone thought she was greedy for eating all that ketchup.

How could she sleep with all these thoughts in her head? She wanted to cry, but she didn't want Ching Ching to hear her. In the bunk below, Ching Ching switched off her lamp.

"Good night, Olivia," she said.

"Good night," said Olivia, hoping her voice sounded normal.

Olivia turned off her lamp, too. The room was very dark now. How long until morning? Olivia rolled on to her side and pretended she was in her own bed. She imagined her own room, her own toys, her own blankets over her. She imagined her mom in the room next door, and it must have worked because very soon she was fast asleep.

CHAPTER *SEVEN*

Olivia had strange dreams. She woke up suddenly, and for a moment she couldn't figure out where she was. The bed was on the wrong side of the room, and up too high, and her pillow smelled funny. It was still dark. She could hear a clock ticking and someone below her breathing.

Oh, yes—she was at Ching Ching's house. She couldn't remember her dream

but she felt wide awake. What time was it?
Definitely too early to get up.

At home, she would have gone to the
bathroom and then maybe crept into her
mom's bed for a cuddle until morning.

That wasn't a good thing to think about
right now. It just made her feel sorry for

herself. Instead, she would think of warm, sleepy things. Hot chocolate before bedtime, sheepskin slippers, the sound of heavy rain on the roof . . .

When Olivia opened her eyes again, it was now Saturday morning. The sunlight was bright through Ching Ching's curtains and the blankets felt too warm.

Olivia listened. The house was still very quiet. Not sleeping quiet, but empty quiet.

She peered over the edge of her bunk bed and looked for Ching Ching. Her bed was a tumble of blankets and sheets, but there was no Ching Ching in it.

Olivia couldn't decide whether to get

up or stay where she was and wait for Ching Ching to come back. Would it be worse to lie in bed for ages and have Ching Ching waiting for her, or worse to go down the hallway and bump into Henry or Daniel or William while she was wearing her pink-and-green pajamas?

She was sitting up in bed, the top of her head almost brushing the ceiling, when Ching Ching appeared at the doorway.

"Oh, you're up," she said. "Good. We have the house to ourselves."

"Where's everyone gone?" asked Olivia.

"The boys play sports on Saturday, so Dad has taken Henry to one field, and Mom has taken Daniel and William to another. They'll be back for lunch, though."

Phew! Olivia could avoid horrible Daniel at least until lunchtime. She climbed down from the bed.

"The boys have eaten all the good cereal," said Ching Ching. "There's only bread left for us."

"Are you allowed to use the stove?" asked Olivia.

"Probably," said Ching Ching. "Why?"

"I could make us French toast. Mom and I make it all the time."

"Cool," said Ching Ching. "That's way better than cereal. What do you need?"

"Eggs, milk, and butter," said Olivia.

"And a frying pan. And bread, of course."

Olivia started mixing the eggs and milk, and soaking the bread.

"While I'm making this," she said, "you should find some cinnamon to go with it."

Ching Ching looked around.

"We don't have any," she said.

"Maple syrup?"

"Nope," said Ching Ching. "What about honey?"

"That will work," said Olivia, dropping the first slice of bread into the frying pan. It sizzled nicely.

"We've got bananas and strawberries, too," said Ching Ching.

"Perfect," said Olivia, turning the toast.

In the end, it was a beautiful breakfast. Olivia cooked two slices of French toast for each of them, and Ching Ching decorated them with honey and slices of fruit.

"Wait," said Ching Ching. "One more thing."

She pulled a can of whipped cream out

of the fridge and squirted a long squiggle onto each plate.

"That," said Olivia, "is so fancy."

"Yeah," said Ching Ching.

"Almost too fancy to eat."

"Yeah," said Ching Ching.

They were quiet for a second, admiring their work. Then Ching Ching caught Olivia's eye and smiled.

"No," she said. "I can eat it."

"Me, too," said Olivia.

They sat by the pool, dangling their legs in the water and eating the toast off plates balanced on their laps.

"This is so nice," said Olivia.

"Yeah," said Ching Ching. "I wish we could do this every Saturday. No boys yelling, no parents nagging."

"Is it nice having a big family?" asked Olivia.

"Mostly. I get tired of being the smallest sometimes, though."

Olivia was the biggest and the smallest rolled into one in her family, but she thought she understood what Ching Ching meant.

"Still," she said. "I bet you don't get bored."

"No," said Ching Ching, eating the last strawberry on her plate.

There was a loud bang from the house

as the front door slammed shut. Then Mrs. Adams yelled out from the backdoor, "Ching Ching!"

"Oh, no," said Ching Ching. "They're back already and we haven't even had our Saturday morning swim yet."

CHAPTER EIGHT

"Ching Ching," said Mrs. Adams, when they were back inside the house. "Have you been using the stove?"

Olivia froze.

In Mrs. Adams's hands were the dirty plates from breakfast, and in the kitchen, sitting in the sink, was the dirty frying pan she had used to cook the French toast.

"No," said Ching Ching.

Olivia couldn't believe her ears. Mrs. Adams looked angry. No, more than angry. She looked wild and fierce.

"Ching Ching," said Mrs. Adams. "Don't lie to me. Have you been using the stove?"

"I promise," said Ching Ching. "I never touched the stove. Did I, Olivia?"

Mrs. Adams turned to Olivia, and Olivia was so frightened, she could hardly breathe.

"Is Ching Ching telling the truth?" asked Mrs. Adams.

"Yes," said Olivia in a shaky voice.

"See?" said Ching Ching to her mom.

"Well, then," said Mrs. Adams. "Who made all this mess?"

"I don't know," said Ching Ching.

She was about to say more, but Olivia spoke up.

"*I* did," Olivia said.

She didn't know what would happen to her now, but she couldn't keep quiet. She would rather die than have Mrs. Adams angry with her, but she never lied to her mom

and didn't know how *not* to tell the truth.

"I used the stove," she said quietly.

Mrs. Adams looked at her. Ching Ching stared at her.

"*You*, Olivia?" said Mrs. Adams.

"I cooked French toast," said Olivia.

She looked at Ching Ching, but her friend's face was a careful blank.

"I see," said Mrs. Adams. "Didn't Ching Ching tell you she isn't allowed to use the stove without a grown-up in the house?"

Olivia shook her head.

"I mean," she said quickly, not wanting to get Ching Ching in trouble, "she thought perhaps it might be all right."

Mrs. Adams sighed and looked at the

two of them.

"I'm sorry to say this, Olivia," she said. "But Ching Ching did not tell you the truth. In this house, children are not allowed to cook on their own."

"I'm sorry," said Olivia, almost in a whisper.

"Ching Ching," said Mrs. Adams, "I'm so angry with you right now. Did you know the stove was left on? When I came in, the burner was glowing red. That's how fires start and houses burn down, and people get very badly hurt."

Ching Ching said nothing.

"Well, what do you have to say for yourself?" asked Mrs. Adams.

"The boys ate all the good cereal," said Ching Ching. "There was nothing else for us to eat."

"That's not quite true, is it?" said Mrs. Adams. "You could have used the toaster. Or the microwave. You could have had banana sandwiches. You could have had milkshakes. You weren't going to starve."

Mrs. Adams opened the fridge to show Ching Ching all the things she could have had for breakfast.

"Look," she said. "Orange juice, watermelon, cheese, tomatoes. You could have had—hey! Did you eat all the straw-berries?"

Oh, no, thought Olivia.

"That's it," said Mrs. Adams, slamming the fridge. "Go to your room now, Ching Ching! I'm just furious."

The two girls fled.

CHAPTER NINE

In Ching Ching's room, Olivia finally started to breathe again.

"I thought your mom was going to kill us," she said.

"She would have if you'd kept talking," said Ching Ching.

"Me?" said Olivia. "What did I do?"

"Only told her everything," said Ching Ching. "If you'd kept quiet, we'd be outside right now, swimming."

Olivia was shocked.

"What are you talking about?" she said. "I left the stove on and we weren't even supposed to touch it!"

"So?" said Ching Ching.

"And you lied to your mom!"

"Sort of," said Ching Ching. "But it wasn't a big lie."

Olivia stared at her friend. She thought Ching Ching was crazy to lie to Mrs. Adams.

Ching Ching sighed.

"Look," she said. "You don't have any brothers or sisters, so you probably don't understand. When you have a big family, you don't need to get into trouble. Mom

and Dad are so busy, and there are so many of us, you can just do what you want. As long as everyone keeps quiet, Mom and Dad can never figure out who did what and so no one gets the blame."

"That's terrible," said Olivia, but she could also see that it was a bit exciting, too.

"But you told on us, so now we have to sit here," said Ching Ching.

"Your mom would have known it was us, though," said Olivia. "We were the only ones home."

"Probably," said Ching Ching. "But then maybe she left with Daniel and William before Dad and Henry left, so maybe it wasn't us after all."

Olivia thought about her place, with just her and her mom. Her mom could tell exactly what Olivia did—every dropped sock, every wet towel, every crumb on the coffee table. Who else could it be?

It was hard to imagine what it would

be like to live in Ching Ching's house. You could get away with so many things!

On the other hand, maybe that made it lonely sometimes. Olivia liked the idea that her mom knew everything about her.

"Anyway," said Ching Ching. "It was worth it. That was the best breakfast I've ever had."

"I can't believe you," said Olivia.

"I know," said Ching Ching. "I'm really, really naughty. But guess what? I'm also full of French toast and strawberries, and I don't care."

Olivia laughed. She couldn't help it. Ching Ching really was terrible, but she was so funny, too. Olivia knew they were stuck in Ching Ching's room because they were in trouble, but right now, giggling with her best friend, even that seemed kind of fun.

CHAPTER TEN

They stayed in Ching Ching's room for ages, reading books and playing with Ching Ching's toys. They heard Mr. Adams come home with Henry, and then all three brothers and Mr. Adams went outside for a swim. Ching Ching and Olivia watched them from the bedroom window.

The boys were diving and doing cannonballs into the pool and water was splashing up in waves all over the sides. Mr. Adams was sitting on the steps in the shallow end, the water up to his chest, cheering the boys on.

"Well done, William!" he called. "That was the biggest splash yet. Watch out, Henry! Daniel's in your way."

"I'm bored now," said Ching Ching. "Don't you think we've been stuck in here long enough?"

"Maybe," said Olivia doubtfully.

In fact, she felt safe in Ching Ching's room. Outside, Mrs. Adams was mad at them, and Daniel might embarrass her again. Who knew what other trouble was waiting?

In here, she had Ching Ching all to herself, and they could play until her mom came to take her home.

"We could do another magazine quiz," she said, but Ching Ching was already opening the bedroom door.

The smell of frying onions drifted in and Ching Ching stood with her head in the hallway, sniffing deeply.

"Oh," she said with longing. "Hamburgers. My favorite."

It seemed like a long time since breakfast, and Olivia's stomach growled.

"I'd love a hamburger," she said. "But my mom's coming to pick me up soon."

"Before lunch or after?" asked Ching

Ching.

"I'm not sure."

"But you will stay for hamburgers, won't you?"

"I hope so," said Olivia, because the smell was getting stronger and more delicious every minute.

"Oops," said Ching Ching, jumping back inside the room and shutting the door. "Mom's coming."

They scurried onto Ching Ching's bed and pretended to be reading books just as Mrs. Adams opened the door.

"OK, you two," she said. "Lunchtime. Olivia, do you know what time your mom is coming to pick you up?"

"No," said Olivia.

"Well, you've got time for a burger, anyway. Your mom can join us if she gets here early. And then," she said more sternly, looking at Ching Ching and the mess in her bedroom, "you can come back here and tidy up a bit."

Lunch was actually fun. They put their hamburgers together on the kitchen table. Olivia tried to make sure Daniel was nowhere near when she got her burger, and she avoided the ketchup, too!

She was just putting some lettuce on her bun and trying to decide whether to have pickles and cheese when someone beside her said, "Do you want some lemonade?"

Olivia looked up and froze. It was Daniel, pouring lemonade into plastic cups. Was he teasing her? Was he being rude somehow? What should she say? Daniel just smiled and passed her a cup.

"Thanks," said Olivia. She didn't know

what else to say.

She suddenly thought that maybe it didn't really matter about the ketchup after all.

She went out with her burger and found Ching Ching sitting under a tree, already eating.

Olivia realized her sleepover was almost over. Part of her felt glad. It would be nice to be back home where she knew all the rules and liked all the food.

Another part of her, though, felt sad because she would miss Ching Ching. She would even miss the things that frightened her—Mrs. Adams when she's angry, Daniel, and the brave and lonely feelings she had sleeping in Ching Ching's top bunk.

Mr. Adams called out from the back door. "Olivia! Look who's here!"

Olivia looked up, and there was her mom. She looked very short next to Mr. Adams, and Olivia had forgotten how pretty she was.

"Oh, no!" said Ching Ching. "Now you'll have to go home, I guess."

"Yeah," said Olivia, and she couldn't tell if she was happy or sad.

They wandered back towards the house.

"Hi, Mom," said Olivia.

"Hi, baby," said her mom.

Olivia didn't want to hug her in front of everybody. Luckily, her mom seemed to know this.

"Did you have a good time?" asked her mom.

"Yeah," said Olivia.

"Did you behave yourself?"

"Um, yeah," said Olivia, looking sideways at Mrs. Adams.

Mrs. Adams laughed.

"She's been a peach," she said. "They've been up to a few tricks, but nothing too terrible."

Olivia smiled with relief.

"Have you packed?" said her mom.

"Not yet."

"Go on, then. I'll stay and chat with Mrs. Adams while you do."

Thanks for having me.

In Ching Ching's room, Olivia found the box of chocolates as she packed her pajamas.

"Oh, I forgot to give these to your mom," she said.

"Let's keep them," said Ching Ching. "Or we could tell Mom she can only have them if she promises you can sleep over next weekend."

"Or you could sleep over at my house," said Olivia. "I could make French toast again for breakfast."

Ching Ching dragged Olivia's bag to the front door. For some reason, it didn't seem to zip up as well as it had the day before. Olivia's pink-and-green pajamas stuck out the top, but now she didn't care who saw them.

"Thank you for having me," she said to Mrs. Adams, giving her the chocolates.

"Oh, lovely," said Mrs. Adams. "These will be even better than strawberries after dinner tonight."

Olivia blushed. She took her bag from Ching Ching and followed her mom out the front door.

"Bye," she said, waving.

She felt happy and brave and somehow more grown-up than yesterday.

"I'm glad you had fun," said her mom as they got into the car.

"Yes," said Olivia. "I really did."

**What will she do when her
sister cuts off her hair?**

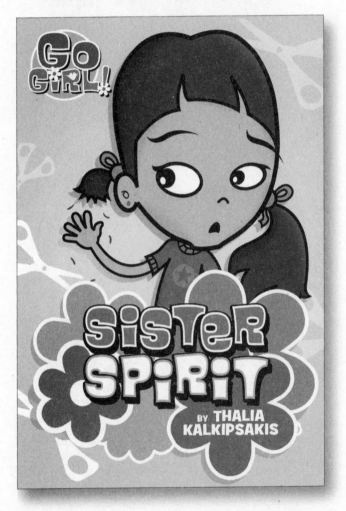

Keep reading for an excerpt!

CHAPTER ONE

My big sister Hannah hates me and I know why. It's because I was born after her.

When Hannah was three, I was born. Everyone said I was *sooooooo cute!* Mom says they stopped saying Hannah was cute, so she threw all my baby clothes down the toilet.

I look younger than I really am. I'm nine years old, but sometimes people think

I look six or seven.

Hannah calls me a baby doll, but she doesn't mean it in a nice way. She says I should try to look my age, but it's not my fault! I can't change how I look.

But now, it's even worse than ever. Hannah cut off my hair and Mom went crazy on her. Then Hannah stopped talking to me.

Strange, isn't it? Hannah cut off my hair and got into trouble, and she blames me for it!

She must really hate me, that girl. Let me explain.

We were watching TV and a show came on about hair. It said that a haircut can change the way you look. It can make you look older or younger.

Hannah said, "Maybe if we cut your hair, people wouldn't think you're so cute anymore!"

"Yeah," I said, not really listening.

Hannah turned off the TV. "Aren't you sick of people saying how cute you look?" she asked.

"Yeah," I said again, but now I *was* listening.

"So why don't we cut your hair short, so you look your age?" Hannah said.

I wasn't sure. It sounded exciting, cutting my hair. I liked the idea of doing something different and looking older. But it's a big

thing to cut off all your hair. And I've had
long hair all my life.

"But what would Mom say?" I said.

"Mom!" Hannah rolled her eyes. Her
hair is dark and shoulder length. It kinks
up around her ears.

"Why do you always worry what Mom

thinks? It's not Mom's hair, " she said.

She had a point. It wasn't Mom's hair, it was *my* hair.

"Come on, let's do it." Hannah's eyes looked bright with excitement.

It was exciting to do something like this together, just her and me. It felt a bit like the stories you read of sisters going shopping and trying on clothes together. It felt good—like Hannah liked me.

It also seemed a little naughty to do something without Mom knowing.

"OK," I said. "Let's do it."

Hannah smiled.

I bet my eyes looked as bright and excited as Hannah's.

When faced with a mean
new girl, will she be a good
friend or be mean, too?

GO GIRL!

THE NEW
GIRL

BY ROWAN
McAULEY

Keep reading for an excerpt!

CHAPTER ONE

One Wednesday morning in the middle of the year, a new girl arrived at Zoe's school. It was the most exciting thing that Zoe could remember happening for ages.

Ms. Kyle knocked on the door during class. Mr. Mack had to stop halfway through a sentence.

Everyone looked up from their books.

"Don't mind us," said Ms. Kyle. "I'm just

talking to Mr. Mack about the new student."

"Wow! A new student," Zoe whispered to her best friend, Iris.

"I know," said Iris. "And what perfect timing. Mr. Mack was speaking way too fast for me to keep up. Quick—while he's still talking to Ms. Kyle—are there two g's in *exaggerated*?"

"Shh," said Zoe. "I'm trying to listen."

But all around her the quiet whispers of the other kids were growing into loud mumblings. She couldn't hear what Ms. Kyle was saying at all.

"Settle down," said Mr. Mack, as Ms. Kyle left. "All right, you all heard that we're getting a new member of our class. Her name is

Isabelle Sinclair, and she will be joining us as soon as she's finished picking up her books and uniform at the office. I know you'll all do your best to make her feel welcome."

Definitely, thought Zoe. *Iris and I will be her best friends.*

"Ok, then," said Mr. Mack. "Let's get back to our vocabulary."

Of course, it was impossible for Zoe to concentrate on her schoolwork. Any minute now, Isabelle could walk through the door. . . .

Zoe wondered what Isabelle would be like. Would she be musical like Iris, funny like Ching Ching, brainy like Chloe, or shy like Olivia?

When Zoe had finished her vocabulary she started drawing little cartoons in the margins of her exercise book. She doodled all the different ways she thought Isabelle might look. Would she be tall or short? Would she have long hair, or—

long hair

short hair

curly hair

"Zoe!" Iris nudged her sharply in the ribs.

Zoe looked up and saw Mr. Mack looking at her pointedly.

"Nice of you to rejoin us, Zoe," he said, dryly.

Zoe quickly sat up straight and covered her drawings with her hand.

"Sorry, Mr. Mack," she said.

Mr. Mack was just about to say something else when there was a knock at the door. It was Ms. Kyle again, followed by a girl in a new school sweater.

Isabelle!

Go Girl!

If you loved this story, don't miss the rest of the series!

THE NEW GIRL
BY ROWAN McAULEY

SLEEP-OVER!
BY ROWAN McAULEY

DANCING QUEEN
BY THALIA KALKIPSAKIS

SISTER SPIRIT
BY THALIA KALKIPSAKIS

THE WORST GYMNAST
BY THALIA KALKIPSAKIS

LUNCHTIME RULES
BY VICKI STEGGALL